Dear Weezie,

Happy

birthday

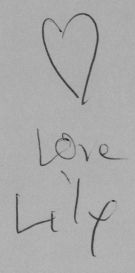

Love
Lily

Doreen Cronin and David Small

Bloom

A
atheneum

A Caitlyn Dlouhy Book

ATHENEUM BOOKS FOR YOUNG READERS

New York London Toronto Sydney New Delhi

O NCE UPON A TIME,

in a beautiful glass kingdom,

there lived an unusual

fairy named Bloom. Her boots

were caked with **mud**.

There was **dirt** between her teeth. **Beetles**

rested in her wings. Bloom's magic could spin sand into glass,

turn weeds into blossoms, and

grow a trickle of rainwater into a racing river.

Bloom was a helpful creature, but her footsteps were

HEAVY,

and she left a trail of tiny

cracks

and **mud** wherever she went.

As the years passed and the kingdom became larger and shinier,
the people cared less about Bloom's magic and noticed only the mess
she left behind. They complained about her

HEAVY feet and her
muddy fingerprints.

Bloom had finally had **enough**. She left without saying good-bye
and went to live in the heart of the forest. Both the kingdom and Bloom
were extraordinarily happy with the choice she had made.

Years and years went by and the glass kingdom had fallen into a state of disrepair. It was held together by duct tape, glue, and peasants. The king was reminded of the powerful creature who once lived in the kingdom. His royal court offered to find her, but the king declined their help. "Surely a creature with such power will answer only to a king."

"Very well, Your Highness, but tread lightly. Fairies are delicate and easily frightened," advised the royal court.

The king entered the forest on his swiftest steed, determined to find the creature and save his kingdom. Bloom felt the horse's hoofbeats and came to greet the king.

"**I** am looking for a magical creature, gone so many years ago," he announced.

"I am here," she answered. The king glanced at Bloom, with her **dirty** hair and **CLUNKY** shoes.

"Show me magic that will save my kingdom," ordered the king.
Bloom placed a bucket of **mud** at the king's feet.

"**H**ow dare you!"
bellowed the king. He dismissed
Bloom as a trickster and rode off.
"Suit yourself," said Bloom, perfectly
happy
to
go
back
to
her
own
business.

When the king returned empty-handed many days later, the queen decided that **she** was **much better suited** to find a magical fairy.

"Maybe your deep voice frightened her off," said the queen reassuringly.

"I must go in your place."

The next day she entered the forest accompanied by a single guard. Bloom heard their footsteps and, once again curious, stepped out to greet the queen.

"I am looking gone so

for a magical creature many years ago,"

announced the queen.

"I am here," answered Bloom.
"Show me the magic that will save
my kingdom," ordered the queen.
Bloom placed a bucket of **mud**
at the queen's feet.

"**How dare you!**"

bellowed the queen. She dismissed
Bloom as a trickster and rode off.
"Have it your way," said Bloom. She picked up her bucket and

skipped

back

to

where

she

came

from.

"What of the magical creature?" asked the king upon the queen's return. Broken glass crunched under her feet as she crossed the room. Rain fell from the cracks in the ceiling.

"Clearly it is too frightened to speak directly with royalty," answered the queen. "We must send someone . . . ordinary."

Genevieve was exactly that—the smallest and q u i e t e s t in the kingdom. Her only job in the palace was to collect, wash, and dry the queen's exquisite crystal sugar spoon. It was the single object in the kingdom that had not yet cracked. The queen summoned Genevieve to her chambers and explained the dire situation.

"You are our last hope," she said kindly.

"I will not fail you, my queen," Genevieve said in her tiny voice.

She brushed the broken glass out of her hair, packed a small bag, and left for the forest.

Genevieve traveled through the dark woods
without carriage or guard. Bloom heard
the sound of her feet pressing into the ground
and stepped out to greet the girl.

"I am looking for a
magical creature, gone
so many years ago,"
said Genevieve.

"I am here!"
said Bloom.

"Have you any magic
to save the kingdom?"

Bloom placed a bucket of **mud** at the girl's feet.

"Perhaps if I explain . . . ,"
said Genevieve.
"You see, our kingdom
is built of glass,
and it is falling to pieces."

Bloom placed a **shovel** at Genevieve's feet.

"I am happy to help you with your chores,
of course, but perhaps you can show me
the magic first?" Genevieve said.

Bloom studied the tiny girl for a moment. She was so delicate, she had barely left a footprint behind her. "What is your work in the kingdom?" asked Bloom.

"I collect, wash, and dry the queen's crystal sugar spoon," Genevieve told her.

"Is that all you can do?"
asked Bloom, hoping she did not sound too harsh.

"Actually . . . I'm not . . . really sure," said Genevieve.
"It's all I am allowed to do, lest my hands get too
rough or too **dirty** to properly
care for the spoon."

"Why would the king and queen send a delicate child,
with such a delicate job, deep into the dark forest
to do something they could not?" asked Bloom.

"Because I am
ordinary,"
answered
Genevieve.

A dark shadow passed over Bloom's face. She picked up her **bucket**.
She picked up her **shovel**. She took the girl by the hand.

"I will show you the magic that can save your kingdom," said Bloom.

Bloom led the girl
into a clearing with
a small house, a
working fire, and
an enormous pit of
mud.

She **plunged** both hands into the pit,

h u r l e d

the brown glob onto the ground,
and quickly made a **mud** pie.

"You try it," said Bloom.

"I musn't!" cried Genevieve. "I'll never be able to touch the queen's sugar spoon again!"

"Do you wish to save the kingdom?" asked Bloom quietly.

Genevieve did not want
to fail the queen.

She closed her eyes,
stuck her hands into the bucket,
and pulled out a scoop of
wet, gloppy earth.

Nervously, she shook her hands,
and the **mud** fell to the ground,
splattering everywhere.

"Not bad!"
said Bloom with a smile.

Genevieve laughed and brushed the **splatters** off her feet.

"Now, try again," Bloom encouraged. This time, Genevieve **enjoyed** the cool, shifting feel of the **mud**, so different from the delicate spoon. She **flung** it to the ground, exactly as Bloom had.

"**N**icely done!" Bloom said.

Smiling, Genevieve shaped the **mud** into a small, round pie.

"**P**erfect!" announced Bloom.

"Now **let's make some magic!**"

Genevieve watched Bloom as she shaped one of the **mud** pies into a perfect brick.

She pulled back her hair with her **muddy** fingers, rolled up her sleeves, and tried to do the same. She made a lopsided, lumpy oval brick.

"You'll get it,**"** said Bloom.

After **sixteen** more tries, Genevieve had made a **perfect** brick.

"What else can I do?"
asked the girl.

"You'll see," said Bloom.

Shovel after shovel, bucket after bucket,

she showed Genevieve how to add straw
into the **mud**. That made the bricks even stronger.
When her pile of bricks towered over her head,
Genevieve was not tired at all,
but eager to do more.

Bloom showed her how
to make mortar,
by mixing mud with sand.

"What's that for?" Genevieve asked.
"You'll see," Bloom told her.

And brick
by
brick,

row by row,

wall
by wall . . .

the fairy and the girl
built a sturdy house
in the middle of the forest.

"I can't believe
what we've
done!"

shouted Genevieve.

"You must go back to the kingdom and share your magic," said Bloom.

"But how can I bring back a house?" asked the girl.

"You can't. You can only tell the king and the queen what you can do," said Bloom.

"They will never believe that an ordinary girl could do such an **extraordinary** thing," Genevieve worried. "What would I tell them?"

"Tell them there is

no such thing as an ordinary girl,"
said Bloom.

Genevieve returned to the kingdom. Her feet were caked in **mud**. There was **dirt** between her teeth. **Beetles** were resting in her hair. She knocked on the palace door and shattered it to pieces.

"I am here!" she shouted.

Then an **ordinary girl** rebuilt a kingdom.

For Julia, Abby, and Samantha
—D. C.

To Sarah, my own beloved garden fairy
—D. S.

A
atheneum

ATHENEUM BOOKS FOR YOUNG READERS
An imprint of Simon & Schuster Children's Publishing Division
1230 Avenue of the Americas, New York, New York 10020
Text copyright © 2016 by Doreen Cronin
Illustrations copyright © 2016 by David Small
All rights reserved, including the right of reproduction in whole
or in part in any form.
ATHENEUM BOOKS FOR YOUNG READERS is a registered trademark
of Simon & Schuster, Inc.
Atheneum logo is a trademark of Simon & Schuster, Inc.
For information about special discounts for bulk purchases, please .
contact Simon & Schuster Special Sales at 1-866-506-1949 or
business@simonandschuster.com.
The Simon & Schuster Speakers Bureau can bring authors to your live event.
For more information or to book an event, contact the Simon & Schuster Speakers
Bureau at 1-866-248-3049 or visit our website at www.simonspeakers.com.
Book design by Ann Bobco
The text for this book is set in Big Caslon.
The illustrations for this book are rendered in ink and watercolor.
Manufactured in the United States of America
0416 PCH
10 9 8 7 6 5 4 3
Library of Congress Cataloging-in-Publication Data
Cronin, Doreen.
Bloom / Doreen Cronin. — First edition.
pages cm
"A Caitlyn Dlouhy Book"
Summary: When the glass kingdom begins cracking, the king and queen
fail in their quest to get help from the fairy Bloom, who can work great magic
but was banished because of her muddy boots and messiness, so they send
Genevieve, an ordinary girl who will do what it takes to save the day.
ISBN 978-1-4424-0620-9 (hardcover)
ISBN 978-1-4814-6005-7 (eBook)
[1. Fairy tales. 2. Fairies—Fiction. 3. Cooperativeness—Fiction. 4. Kings; queens,
rulers, etc.—Fiction. 5. Magic—Fiction.] I. Title.
PZ8.C8688Blo 2016
[E]—dc23   2015002029